EMERGING
NATIONS

TURKEY

PHILIP STEELE

A+

Smart Apple Media

EMERGING NATIONS

TURKEY

A⁺

Smart Apple Media

Published by Smart Apple Media, an imprint of Black Rabbit Books
P.O. Box 3263, Mankato, Minnesota 56002
www.blackrabbitbooks.com

Published by arrangement with the Watts Publishing Group LTD, London.

Cataloging-in-Publication Data is available from the Library of Congress
ISBN 978-1-59920-991-3 (library binding)
ISBN 978-1-62588-605-7 (eBook)

Series Editor: Julia Bird
Series Advisor: Emma Epsley, geography teacher and consultant
Series Design: sprout.uk.com

Photo credits:
AFP/Getty Images: 9. Walter Allgower/Alamy: 13. Adem Altan/AFP/Getty Images: 10, 29b.
Angelmaker/Dreamstime: 19t. Archives du 7e Art Zeynofilm/Photos12/Alamy: 35t.
Bart Pro/Alamy: 18b. Tibor Bognar/Alamy: 42. Orhan Cam/Shutterstock: 12.
Caro/Alamy: 16, 40. Mehmet Cetin/Shutterstock: 6. Mike Cohen/Shutterstock: 34.
Kobby Dagan/Dreamstime: 22. Elfred/Shutterstock: 43b. Faraways/Shutterstock: 28, 32.
Jeremy Graham/Alamy: 14t. Sadik Gulec/Shutterstock: 11b, 14b, 25b, 43t. Haytham Pictures/Alamy: 41b.
Images & Stories/Alamy: 39b. Mykola Irashchenko/Shutterstock: 27. Svetlana Jafarova/Shutterstock: 18t.
JM Travel Photography/Shutterstock: 21t. Kevin Landwer-Johan/istockphoto: 39r. Evren Kalinbacak/Shutterstock: 25t, 38.
Timothy Large /Shutterstock: 21b. Lonely Planet Images/Getty Images: 24b. LOOK Die Bildagentur der Fotografen GmbH/
Alamy: 19bl. Viacheslav Lopatin/Shutterstock: 15t. Tina Lorien/istockphoto: 33b. mehmetcan/Shutterstock: 37.
Melis/Shutterstock: 35b. Muratart/Shutterstock: 24t. Alexander Nemenov/Getty Images: 26b.
Ho New/Reuters: 31b. nexus7/Shutterstock: front cover b, 3b, 15br. 1001nights/istockphoto: 26t.
Petitfrere/Dreamstime: 17t, Paul Prescott/Shutterstock: 31t. Red Diplomat/istockphoto: 19br.
Joe Restuccia III/Alamy: 23b. Pascal Saez/Alamy: 36t. Alex Segre/Alamy: 39tl. Valery Shanin/Shutterstock: 20.
Alexey Stoganov/istockphoto: 17b. Boris Stroujko/Shutterstock: 23t. David Sutherland/Alamy: 11t.
Marco Tomasini/Shutterstock: 36b. Alexander A Trofimov//Shutterstock: 33t. Typhoonski/Dreamstime: front cover t, 3t.
Martyn Unsworth/Dreamstime: 7c. Paul Vinten/Shutterstock: 15bl. Janine Wiedel/Photolibrary/Alamy: 30.

Printed in the United States by CG Book Printers
North Mankato, Minnesota

PO 1721
3-2015

987654321

EMERGING NATIONS

TURKEY

CONTENTS

CHAPTER 1:
INTRODUCING TURKEY
EAST MEETS WEST

BRIDGING THE BOSPHORUS

On one side is Europe. On the other is Asia. Between these two continents lies a narrow strip of blue sea. This is the Bosphorus, 19 miles (31 km) in length and just 0.2 mile (0.4 km) to 1.1 mile (1.8 km) across. The Bosphorus Strait links the Black Sea with the Sea of Marmara and is the gateway to Istanbul, Turkey's largest city. For thousands of years, passengers could cross the Bosphorus only by boat. Today, two great suspension bridges span it, and a third one is under construction. Times are changing in Turkey.

WELCOME TO TURKEY

European Turkey is made up of a small corner of land, known as Eastern Thrace (Doğu Trakya), and is bordered by Greece and Bulgaria. Most of Turkey—about 97 percent of the total area—lies in Asia. The Anatolia region (Anadolu) stretches eastward toward Georgia, Armenia, Iran, Iraq, and Syria. This is a land of hot summers. Winters are mild along the coasts, but can be bitterly cold in the interior. It is a land of mountains, windswept plateaus, and long coastlines. Turkey also has a constant risk of earthquakes—Turkey lies over an active geological area.

The Fatih Sultan Mehmet Bridge crosses the Bosphorus Strait. It links the European and Asian sides of the city. During rush hour it is busy with commuter traffic.

UKRAINE

RUSSIAN FEDERATION

BULGARIA

Black Sea

GEORGIA

AZERBAIJAN

THRACE
REECE

Edirne

Bosphorus

Istanbul
Sea of Marmara Izmit

Bursa

Adapazan

Ankara

Eskişehir

Samsun

PONTIC MTS

ARMENIA

River Euphrates Erzurum

ARARAT (5,137m)

TURKEY

ANATOLIA

River Kızılırmak

Kayseri

Malatya

Diyarbak
River Tigris

IRAN

Aegean Sea

Izmir

Denizil

Konya

CAPPADOCIA

Kahramamaraş
Gaziantep

TAURUS MTS Mersin

Adana

Antakya

SYRIA

IRAQ

CYPRUS

Mediterranean Sea LEBANON

Dawn lights up the ancient rock citadel of Üchisar, which is the highest point in Cappadocia.

NEW DIRECTIONS

Turkey's economy has been racing ahead. Some experts say that by 2023 it could be among the world's top 10. Other economists believe that problems may lie ahead. Many political questions are being asked. What kind of country is Turkey turning into? Will Turkey's newfound wealth benefit the poor as well as the rich? What kind of nation is this new Turkey?

Is it a religious, Islamic country? Or a secular one, in which faith and politics are kept apart? Is it a country that respects the human rights of its minority people? What part will Turkey play in the turbulent politics of the Middle East region as a whole? Will it become a member of the European Union (EU) as planned? As it straddles the Bosphorus, should Turkey be looking eastward into Asia or westward into Europe? Or should Turkey act as bridge builder between the east and west?

SPOTLIGHT ON TURKEY

FULL NAME: Republic of Turkey • AREA: 303,000 square miles (784,000 sq km) • POPULATION: 81,619,392 • CAPITAL: Ankara (pop. 3.85 million) • BIGGEST CITY: Istanbul (pop. 14.2 million) • LONGEST RIVER: Kızılırmak 842 miles (1,355 km) • HIGHEST MOUNTAIN: Ağrı (Ararat) 16,854 feet (5,137 m) • RESOURCES: Bauxite, chromite, copper, iron ore, coal, oil, natural gas, boron salts

CHAPTER 2:
THE NATION
A RICH HISTORY

Ottoman troops invaded Europe and besieged Vienna in 1529 and 1683. This old painting shows troops capturing a Hungarian town in 1543.

ANCIENT LANDS

The remains of ancient civilizations lie in the rocks and dry soil of Turkey. Anatolia (see page 6) played an important part in the early development of farming, town-building, and ironworking. In the west and along the Aegean coast, one can see the ruins of ancient Troy and fine cities of the classical world. Byzantium, an ancient Greek settlement on the Bosphorus, became the eastern capital of the Roman Empire in 330 AD. Constantinople was the capital of the medieval Byzantine Empire and a center of Christianity. Trade brought the riches of Asia through its ports.

TURKISH SULTANS

Turkish peoples originally came from Central Asia. Many invaded the Middle East in the Middle Ages (fifth through fifteenth centuries AD) and adopted the Muslim faith. One group of Turks, the Seljuks, advanced from Persia (Iran) into Anatolia. Seljuks were followed by another group, known as the Osmanli or Ottomans, who captured Constantinople in 1453. The city became known as Istanbul from the Greek words for "in the city." Beautiful mosques were built and Turkish sultans ruled in splendor from their palace beside the Bosphorus. Their empire extended across the Middle East, North Africa, Greece, and southeastern Europe.

DECLINE AND FALL

Ottoman power declined as Western European nations became ever more powerful. In 1914, the Ottoman Empire entered World War I on the side of Germany, hoping to win back lost territories. By 1918, it had lost everything. The winners carved up the former empire and a Greek invasion sparked off a bitter war of independence. The last sultan, Mehmet VI, was overthrown in 1922.

A NEW REPUBLIC

In 1923, the capital was moved to Ankara, more centrally located in Anatolia. A new Turkish republic was founded. Its first president was an army officer, Mustafa Kemal, known as Atatürk ("Father of the Turks"). Atatürk was an authoritarian leader and a stern nationalist. Cutting all ties with the past, he brought in reforms to create a secular, modern European-style state. He died in 1938, but his Republican People's Party (CHP) continued to rule until 1950. The country's first democratic election handed power to the right-wing Democratic Party. The Turkish military repeatedly intervened in politics in 1960, 1971, and again in 1980. Democracy returned to Turkey in 1983 with struggles between left and right, as well as widespread corruption in an improving, developing economy.

Mustafa Kemal Atatürk was the founder of modern Turkey. Masks of his face were worn to mark the anniversary of his death.

PEOPLE AND LANGUAGES

GROWING FAST

Approximately 81 million people live in Turkey. The population is growing each year at a rate of about 1.2 percent, higher than in most of Europe. The effects of this are felt chiefly around the big cities of Istanbul and Ankara, as well as in coastal areas.

MEET THE TURKS

Approximately 75 percent of the population are ethnic Turks. Many are descendants of the Turks who settled here in the Middle Ages and are very proud of their history, culture, and identity. Related Turkic peoples live across Central Asia, Russia, and China. The Turkish language, *Türkçe*, is spoken throughout the country and has official status.

OTHER CITIZENS

As many as 22 other ethnic groups live in Turkey. For much of its history, Turkey has tried to make sure that these citizens see themselves as Turks above all else, with governments suppressing minority cultures. Today, steps are being taken to improve minority relations. Some Turkish citizens, such as Greeks and Armenians, belong to peoples who have historic grievances with the Turks. Armenians revolted against Ottoman rule from the 1890s and between 1915 and 1923. More than a million were massacred by the Turks. Turkish governments have repeatedly rejected accusations that this was genocide.

Young women wave Turkey's national flag at a rally to mark National Youth and Sports Day.

A QUESTION OF DRESS

Beautiful traditional costumes may be worn at regional and historical festivals, but Turkish people generally wear typical European dress. About half of the women may also wear the *tesettür*, a simple headscarf or hijab, according to Islamic beliefs about modesty. The wearing of head coverings and full veils in schools and other public buildings was forbidden by Atatürk's secular reforms. But in 2012, the classroom ban on headscarves was lifted. This was very controversial, and the issue is still the subject of intense debate for political as well as religious reasons.

PEACE FOR THE KURDS?

The Kurdish people live in Turkey, Syria, Iraq, and Iran. Their wish for self-government has led to many years of conflict. In Turkey, Kurds make up about 18 percent of the population. Most live in the mountainous east and speak dialects of the Kurdish language. Over the ages, Kurdish identity and language have been suppressed. This led to protests and the formation of pro-Kurdish political parties, some peaceful and some violent. An armed rising began in 1984 dominated by the PKK (Kurdistan Workers' Party). Decades of bombings and attacks by the rebels were met by fierce reprisals, discrimination, and human rights abuses. Tens of thousands died and hundreds of thousands were made homeless. In 2013, Abdullah Ocalan, the jailed PKK leader, declared a ceasefire. This breakthrough suggests both sides are now searching for peace.

A protest in Istanbul commemorates the bombing of Kurds by Turkish air force jets at Uludere in 2011. Most of the 34 dead were unarmed teenagers.

11

ANKARA POLITICS

CENTER OF GOVERNMENT

As a democratic republic, Turkey's people can vote from the age of 18. It is divided into 81 provinces (*iller*). The national capital is the city of Ankara, which is also the center of government.

A NEW SYSTEM?

Until 2014, members of Turkey's parliament elected the nation's president. That year, Recep Tayyip Erdoğan became the first Turkish president chosen by the citizens in a direct election. The president serves a five-year term and may be reelected only once. Before he was elected president, Erdoğan was Turkey's prime minister. While the president makes sure Turkey's constitution is upheld, the prime minister leads the government. After Erdoğan was elected president, his political party elected Ahmet Davutoğlu as president. Davutoğlu is an Erdoğan loyalist. Some Turks worried that this meant Erdoğan would continue to control the prime minister's office through Davutoğlu.

ELECTION TIME

The parliament, or *Meclis,* is called the Grand National Assembly. It has a single chamber with 550 seats. Turkey has no fewer than 61 political parties at the current count. Erdoğan and Davutoğlu's AKP (Justice & Development Party) is conservative, favoring the "free market" and moderate Islamic values. The second biggest party, the CHP (Republican People's Party), is social democratic, secular, and Kemalist. Smaller parties include far-right nationalists, pro-Kurdish parties, socialists, communists, liberals, and Greens.

Ankara is Turkey's capital, its seat of government, and the second largest city after Istanbul.

WHAT'S THE AGENDA?

More than any other, it is President Erdoğan who has shaped the new Turkey. What impact have his policies had? Although the economy has grown dramatically, many people remain poor. Progress toward becoming a full member of the European Union (EU) has been unsteady. However, meeting the conditions for EU membership has improved Turkey's human rights record in some areas. At times, Erdoğan's AKP has clashed head on with the military by accusing them of plotting yet another takeover. These charges have been rejected by the army and their supporters, who see themselves as guardians of a secular future. Erdoğan's proposed changes to the constitution have stirred up another issue. There is little doubt that he is not only controversial, but also an effective politician with an instinct for survival.

Banners proclaim then-Prime Minister Erdoğan's popularity. But dramatic protests in Istanbul in summer 2013 showed that many Turks mistrust his desire for more power and his hardline tactics.

FOCUS ON ISTANBUL: THE GREAT CITY

THE GREAT CITY

This city has had many names in its history—Byzantium, Constantinople, Istanbul. The same conditions that brought it success in ancient times still make it great today. Its geographical position places it at a crossroads of trading routes, communications, and cultures. Ankara may no longer have its status as the capital, but Istanbul remains at the commercial and cultural heart of Turkey.

The wider urban area now covers 2,063 square miles (5,343 sq km) with a population of about 13.9 million. That is an increase of 10 times since the 1950s, just one example of the many changes sweeping across Turkey.

HEART OF THE CITY

Istanbul rises from the sea with an inlet called the Golden Horn forming a natural harbor. Roman and Byzantine ruins can still be seen, and the stone minarets of Ottoman mosques soar above the skyline. But Istanbul is no mere museum; it is full of life. The city dwellers (known as *Stamboullou*) shop, chat, buy, and sell. The sounds of the city—traffic, car horns, music, loudspeakers—call faithful Muslims to prayer five times daily. Tourists take boat trips, throng the restaurants around Taksim Square, or dance at the nightclubs of Beyoğlu.

What keeps Istanbul going? Çay—a sweet black tea, served in a small glass. It is part of every business deal, every commercial transaction, every social occasion.

Nearly 1,500 years old, the impressive Christian Church of Hagia Sophia ("Holy Wisdom") later became a mosque and is now a museum.

The Galata Bridge crosses the Golden Horn. It links the old city district of Sultanahmet with the Karaköy district, known for its shops, markets, and restaurants.

The Sapphire building, a symbol of change in Istanbul's Levent district is one of the tallest buildings in Turkey. It includes shops and luxury apartments.

With multiple domes, the Sultanahmet Camii is known as the Blue Mosque in English because of the beautiful blue ceiling tiles inside. Its minarets look out over the Bosphorus.

WORK AND LAND
WORK AND INDUSTRY

ON THE UP?

Turkey is emerging as a big player in world economics. In 2011, its growth rate hit 8.5 percent, making it the fastest developing nation in Europe. In 2012, the rate dropped to about 3 percent, but even this lower figure was better than Europe's more developed nations, where financial crises brought growth to a near standstill. One forecast for 2016 is 3.9 percent. Whether Turkey's success is sustainable in the longer term, however, remains to be seen.

Stock exchange traders wheel and deal in Istanbul. In 2013, all Turkish exchanges were brought together under a single corporation called Borsa Istanbul.

DOING BUSINESS

Almost half of the Turkish workers are employed in service industries. These include a strong banking and financial sector, and a successful tourist industry. The manufacturing sector provides jobs for 26 percent of the workforce. Turkish workers produce household appliances, electronic equipment, cars, ships, garments, textiles, and food products such as olive oil. Turkey's trading partners include Germany and other European Union countries, plus Russia, Iraq, Iran, and China.

TAKE-HOME WAGES

The Turkish currency is called the lira. So how much do people in Turkey earn? The legal minimum wage from 2013 was 804 lira ($378) per month. The Turkish trade unions point out that this is well below what they regard as a living wage. The average income in Turkey after tax in 2013 was 1,410 lira ($663) per month. That would be the typical payment to a teacher, for example, before overtime is added on. A laborer or cleaner might make 1,200 lira ($564), while management pay scales are similar to those in other European countries.

RESOURCES

Turkey has reserves of most major metals. It also has oil and natural gas, but Turkey still has to import more of these fuels to meet its needs. Pipelines link Turkey with Azerbaijan, Russia, and Iran. A proposed extension may soon carry gas westward to Austria as well.

WIN OR LOSE?

President Erdoğan has introduced capitalist, free-market economic policies, with many state-run enterprises such as power plants being privatized. Such policies have delivered wealth and growth, but this has increased the gap between rich and poor. A gender gap exists, too. Across the EU, about 65 percent of women work. But in Turkey only 25 percent of women work, and many of those are in low-paid jobs.

From tree to production line. Workers process olives at a factory in Akhisar in the Aegean region.

An international tour guide addresses her customers. Erdoğan has urged women to have more babies, which, of course, limits their working opportunities.

The old way of doing business in Istanbul can be seen at its Grand Bazaar or Kapalı Çarşı. It is the biggest market of its kind in the world with 61 covered streets and about 4,000 shops, cafés, and banks. Street names still show how merchants were grouped together by their trade. Today, the bazaar still looks like a treasure house of gleaming copper, oriental carpets, jewelery, and cloth, and draws in millions of tourists.

MONEY MAKER

Istanbul has always been about making money. Today this city alone produces more than one-quarter of Turkey's gross domestic product (GDP). It is the financial capital and is home to the headquarters of Turkish and international banks and corporations. The chief business districts are Levent and Maslak. Outer districts are industrial, processing food or producing textiles, electronics, and petrochemicals.

PEOPLE AT WORK

More than half of Istanbul's labor force works in services, and many of them in the tourist industry. Other employers include universities, hospitals, banks, call centers, and utility services. Although the city has a large number of billionaires, it also has Turkey's highest unemployment rate. The gap between rich and poor is strikingly visible.

The Grand Bazaar has been located on this site in the Fatih district since 1461. It has survived fires and earthquakes over the centuries. The covered market offered security to the city's traders, where their wares could be locked up and guarded by night.

The Kadiköy district on the Asian side of Istanbul is famous for its fresh fish and seafood, available in small restaurants and bustling markets.

The skyline of Istanbul's modern business districts towers above the old city and the seashore, and is a symbol of the nation's rapid economic growth.

Istanbul road workers take a break during the evening rush hour.

Washing is hung out to dry on old houses in Balat. Once it was a poorer district that was home to Jews and Greeks. It is now being restored and is attracting new money.

19

THE GROWING CITIES

URBAN HOTSPOTS

Istanbul and Ankara may be Turkey's top two cities, but many others are growing rapidly. Izmir, on the Aegean coast, has a population of well over 3 million. Bursa, Adana, Gaziantep, Konya, Anatalya, and Kayseri are all big residential or industrial centers. Their streets are jammed with noisy traffic and thronged with shoppers.

In ancient times, Izmir was known as Smyrna. Industrialization and a massive population increase transformed this city in the later 20th century.

THE URBAN SWITCH

It was not always like this. In 1935, over 75 percent of Turks were still village dwellers. Fast forward to today, and we find nearly the same proportion of the population is now living in towns and cities. Urbanization is still increasing by 1.7 percent each year. It has been caused chiefly by industrial development. Factories and other workplaces offer better, more secure wages and an easier life than working on the land.

Wooden housing in the traditional style can still be seen in corners of Istanbul.

NEIGHBORHOODS

Traditional Turkish cities always have had a strong sense of neighborhood. You can see this in older city districts that often surround a mosque. You may see wooden housing in the Ottoman style, with tiled roofs, projecting upper floors, courtyards, squares, local markets, cafés, and alleyways. However, modern housing and commercial developments of brick and concrete tend to sprawl out and engulf old neighborhoods. This destroys a sense of community. Critics say that profit now comes before people and heritage. Large numbers of people live in the unplanned substandard housing that caters to the urban poor or rural migrants seeking work.

SOCIAL IMPACT

As in other rapidly developing countries, urbanization has helped economic growth, but this has come at a price. Towns have struggled to cope with the flood of people in need of services and affordable housing. Women who previously worked informally on family farms have found it harder to find work in the cities. City life also tends to fragment the wider family connections and networks of support that have always been common in the countryside.

Housing blocks have sprung up across Turkey in recent years.

21

FIELDS AND VILLAGES

FIELDS AND VILLAGES

Olive groves and fields of sunflowers border the Aegean coast. Sheep graze the grasslands of central Anatolia. Cherries and hazelnuts thrive in the Black Sea region of the north, where dairy cattle provide milk and cream. The Turkish landscape is varied, beautiful, and, in the more fertile regions, very productive. Nearly 30 percent of the land is arable (suitable for agriculture).

Sunflowers have been a major crop since the 1920s, especially in European Turkey. Their seeds are processed to make vegetable oil.

RURAL COMMUNITIES

Life in small villages is still based on traditions of extended family groupings. However, things are changing. With more tractors and combine harvesters, fewer laborers are in the fields. The removal of farming subsidies by the Erdoğan government also has made many small farmers decide to quit. The tide of rural workers into the cities has become a flood.

Life on the land has often been hard in the past. But in many ways, it has become easier with better water, electricity, and communications. Agriculture still employs over a quarter of Turkey's workforce and brings in about 9 percent of national gross domestic product (GDP).

COUNTRY HOME

Housing in Turkey's villages can be made of wood, stone, or concrete. Many buildings have white walls and red-tiled roofs. In the Cappadoccia region, some traditional housing was carved from rocks and caves which are now a popular tourist attraction. Many houses are still set into the local limestone rock formations.

CROPS AND HARVESTS

Turkey is self-sufficent in farming produce. Turkish farmers grow wheat, rye, and barley, as well as root crops such as potatoes and sugar beets. Tomatoes, cucumbers, eggplants, and peppers are also popular crops. The climate is perfect for growing melons, nuts such as almonds and pistachios, and fruits such as figs, apricots, apples, quinces, lemons, grapefruit, and pomegranates. The olive is native to the region, and Turkey is estimated to have about 85 million trees—some of them hundreds of years old. Grapes are cultivated for making wine, and tea plantations provide çay tea (see page 14). Beehives yield golden, fragrant honey—a common breakfast treat.

Ancient rock housing in the Nevşehir province of Central Anatolia.

LAND AND SEA

Turkey produces cotton and wool for its textile industries. Sheep and goats are raised in the plateau, grasslands, and mountains. Along the coasts, fishing boats bring in tuna, sardines, anchovies, and squid.

Village women collect the potato harvest in the hot sun.

ON THE MOVE

VITAL LINK

Turkey covers an area slightly larger than Texas. The journey across Turkey from west to east is about 1,100 miles (1,700 km). Over the ages, the country's mountainous regions have slowed travel and communications. As Turkey always has provided the chief overland route between Asia and Europe, good transport infrastructure is key to future success.

ROAD AND RAIL

Intercity road networks are being improved in the west. Turkey has 40,776 miles (65,623 km) of roads, 89 percent are paved. Most of the roads are of motorway-standard and mostly toll roads. Turks own about 15 million vehicles, and car ownership is growing rapidly. The main car manufacturers are Ford-Otosan,

A train crosses the spectacular Varda viaduct in Adana province. This 320-foot (98-m) high bridge was built by German engineers in 1916.

Long-distance trucks line up at a border post. Turkey lies on the overland trading route between Europe and Asian countries, such as Iran, Pakistan, and India.

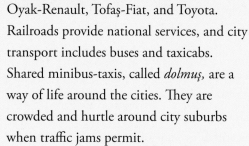

Oyak-Renault, Tofaş-Fiat, and Toyota. Railroads provide national services, and city transport includes buses and taxicabs. Shared minibus-taxis, called *dolmuş,* are a way of life around the cities. They are crowded and hurtle around city suburbs when traffic jams permit.

About 6,835 miles (11,000 km) of track make up the TCDD (Turkish State Railways) rail network, which connects the Turkish regions. It also takes passengers eastward to Iran via a train ferry across Lake Van. New high-speed rail links are being constructed in the west to provide a speedier service between Istanbul and Ankara.

SEA AND AIR

Shipping plays a crucial part in the Turkish economy, and large cargo ships pass under the Bosphorus bridges every day. The major container ports are Haydarpaşa, Ambarlı, Izmir, and Mersin. Ferries are also important as they carry local passengers and tourists around Turkey's coasts and lakes. Turkey has 88 airports; external and internal air travel is growing fast. The chief air hub is Atatürk International at Yesilyurt, the largest airport for Istanbul.

A Turkish Airlines Airbus takes off from Istanbul's Atatürk International airport.

The 9-mile (14-km) rail tunnel under the Bosphorus took nine years to build and opened in 2013.

TUNNEL TO THE FUTURE?

Approximately 12 million people journey in and around Istanbul every day. This has increased pollution and delay.

- The Marmaray project is one solution. This involves upgrading suburban rail and rapid transit networks to get traffic off the roads. A rail tunnel was built under the Bosphorus strait. The sunken, earthquake-proof tube is now the deepest tunnel of this type in the world. At one point, it reaches 200 feet (60 m) below sea level.

- The project ran years behind schedule largely due to the discovery of a huge Byzantine-era archaeological site close to the excavations. It finally opened on October 29, 2013, the 90th anniversary of the founding of the Turkish republic.

AGAINST NATURE?

URBAN HAZE

In cities such as Istanbul, Ankara, Bursa, and Erzurum, a hazy smog often hangs in the air. During cold winters, the smoke from heating fuels may add to this. The building of new factories, the growth of big cities, and the increase in traffic exhaust fumes have made the air more polluted. Economic development often comes at a high cost to the environment.

Clearing up the beaches after an oil spill. The Black Sea coast has suffered repeatedly from accidents at sea.

As the city of Istanbul spreads outward, the air becomes polluted and the natural environment is destroyed.

POLLUTION AND DEFORESTATION

Turkey's coasts are at risk of oil spills and pollution, especially at busy shipping bottlenecks such as the Straits of the Bosphorus and the Dardanelles in northwestern Turkey. The Black Sea, almost enclosed by land, has absorbed industrial, chemical, radioactive, and human waste from the surrounding countries. Farmland has seen the overuse of fertilizers. In many areas, land has been over-grazed by herds. Deforestation has also degraded the land. The removal of tree roots, which trap moisture, can create a dust bowl. As much as 69 percent of the country has suffered from soil erosion.

The magnificent cinereous vulture is endangered due to deforestation and poisoning.

DINNER TIME FOR VULTURES

Vultures are having a hard time worldwide. Often they are poisoned by veterinary chemicals in the dead livestock that they scavenge. Some of Turkey's vulture species are also under threat. In the far east of Anatolia, at Iğdir on the Armenian border, conservationists have created a popular feeding place for the birds. Roadkill, butchers' scraps, or farm animals that have died of natural causes provide food for vultures. This makes it possible for the public to view and photograph these big birds as they feed. Some of the vultures are fitted with transmitters. This allows satellites to track their migration patterns.

THE ENERGY DEBATE

Fossil fuels such as oil, gas, and coal are polluters. Turkey uses these to generate the vast majority of its energy. The government is planning a new nuclear power program, but a proposed plant at Akkuyu in Mersin province has aroused opposition due to safety concerns. One possible source of more energy is hydroelectric. But the building of new dams has also been controversial. It puts the environment and communities at risk and potentially reduces the water supply to neighboring Syria, Iraq, and Georgia. Plans are underway to increase wind and geothermal power. It has a target of 30 percent of total energy coming from renewable sources by 2023.

PROTECTING WILDLIFE

A lot is at stake. Turkey is on major migration routes for birds; its varied landscapes are a precious world resource. These include forests, steppes, mountains, wetlands, coasts, and seas. These ecosystems support a diverse range of plants and animals. These include brown bears, wolves, lynxes, and many other creatures that are at risk from hunting as well as loss of their habitat. Attempts to improve wildlife conservation are up against relaxed planning laws that were designed to encourage mining and the building of tourist resorts.

CHAPTER 4:
TURKISH SOCIETY
SEEKING JUSTICE

HUMAN RIGHTS

Criticisms of social justice in Turkey have been raised at many points in its history. Turkey has had to meet various conditions as a result of its application for EU membership, which has brought about improvements. Even so, the United Nations and watchdogs such as Amnesty International and Human Rights Watch still raise concerns. There are accusations of laws not being enforced and a lack of accountability. Victims of injustice have included refugees, asylum seekers, gays, migrant workers, and the poor.

TAKSIM SUMMER

In May 2013, a protest in Istanbul's Taksim Gezi Park dominated news headlines. It began with a small protest about urban development. Soon, it spread to other cities. The confrontation was between the protestors on one side and the police and Prime Minister Erdoğan on the other. The issues in dispute included the right of assembly, freedom of the press, free speech, and the protection of Turkey's secular constitution. Protestors were treated harshly. The extent of opposition to Erdoğan's authority was now clear. Was he losing touch?

These protestors in Istanbul were made up of many different factions that united against a number of different government policies.

CEYLAN'S STORY

Turkish women won the vote in the 1930s. In 1933, Tansu Çiller was the first elected female prime minister. Women are prominent in public life. However, violence against women is widespread in modern cities as well as in remote rural areas. Some regions believe in "honor killings." If a woman marries against the wishes of her parents, she is killed by her family or forced to commit suicide.

The case of Ceylan Sosyal, a 19-year-old woman from Hatay province, shocked Turkey in 2011. After an unapproved marriage, Ceylan's new husband abandoned her. She was then murdered by her brother. This tragedy resulted in vocal campaigns against violence toward women. In 2013, Turkey's parliamentary Constitution Commission added guarantees of protection against domestic violence and early and forced marriage.

Ceylan Sosyal, victim of a horrific "honor killing."

LAW AND ORDER

The Turkish police is the chief agency for law enforcement. Blue-and-white police uniforms and patrol cars are a familiar sight on city streets. The gendarmerie, a military-trained body, carries out most rural policing. Turkey's legal system is influenced by various European models. It is based on the 1982 constitution which was reformed in 1991 and 2004. Judges are independent from the government. Turkey has civil and criminal courts and separate courts for military, constitutional, and state security matters. The latter often attract political controversy dealing with organized crime, terrorism, and sedition. Jail conditions have been criticized by human rights organizations, but no death sentences have been passed since 2004.

The number of prisoners in Turkey have more than doubled between 2004 and 2013.

HEALTH AND EDUCATION

STARTING SCHOOL

At about 8:15 each morning, children line up in rows and then file into the schoolroom under a portrait of Kemal Atatürk. As the founder of the modern Turkish republic, he was the first to bring a rational—and national—approach to education in Turkey. Since then, the period in which children have to attend school has been extended from 5 to 8 years, and again to 12 years, between the ages of 6 and 18. Schooling is divided into three stages: four years at primary (first level), four years at primary (second level), and four years at secondary. In addition, children may have preschool education or go on to study at a college or university.

WHAT KIND OF EDUCATION?

Teachers in Turkey have always taught pupils to learn things by memorization. Now, a new curriculum plans to place children at the center of the learning process. However, funding may be needed to bring real change. Turkey currently spends about 3 percent of its GDP on education. This is much the same as Russia, but lower than most EU countries. The education system is run by the state, but Turkey also has some private schools. Almost all men (98 percent) can read and write, but just under 92 percent of women are literate. In some rural areas it is still difficult to get families to send their girls to school.

A teacher helps children with their class work. Secondary pupils have six lessons lasting 40 minutes each school day.

More than 6 percent of the Turkish population is over 65 years old.

PUBLIC HEALTH

How long can you expect to live? In Turkey, the average figures are nearly 73 years for a male and 79 for a female. Common health problems include cancer, heart disease, stroke, and infectious diseases. In recent years, the improvement of water supplies and a public smoking ban show that practical steps are being taken toward improvements in public health. Turkey has 1.7 doctors and 2.5 hospital beds per 1,000 of the population. These statistics compare with 2.5 and 2.9 respectively in the United States. A growing number of overseas visitors travel to Turkey for medical treatment. Beginning in 2003, Erdoğan set about privatizing the state healthcare system. His reforms have been welcomed by some, but they have also attracted criticism and protests.

A hospital nurse hands a newborn baby to its happy mother. Home births are more common in rural areas.

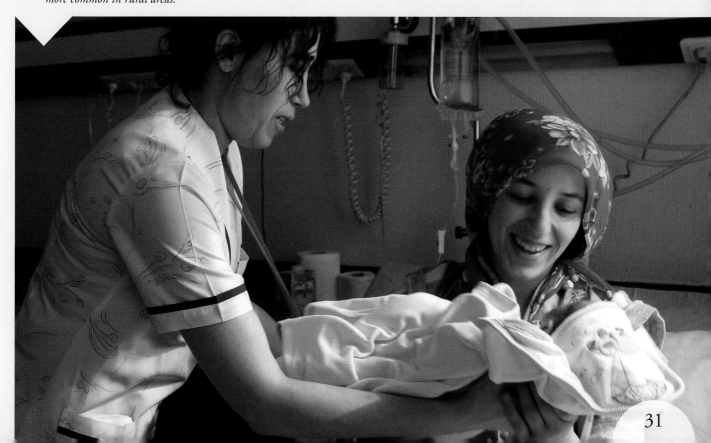

31

MEDIA TALK

Readers can choose from a wide range of newspapers. These range from the conservative Zaman *to the more left-wing* Posta.

CHANGING TIMES

Turkish media, as elsewhere, is going through a period of rapid change. In the old days, the press was dominated by big corporations that had close relations with the government and the military and supported their agendas. In recent years, large sections of the media have been bought up by business leaders who sympathize with the privatizing program of the Erdoğan government.

SATELLITE DISHES

Television reaches about 18 million Turkish households as satellite dishes beam in a multitude of channels. TRT still has a large share of the TV and radio audience. This network also provides a Kurdish-language service. Interest is growing in Turkish-made programs rather than imports. Even these can cause political upset. In 2012, a popular drama called *Muhteşem Yüzyıl* (*Magnificent Century*) was fiercely attacked by Prime Minister Erdoğan for its portrayal of the most famous Ottoman sultan, Suleiman the Magnificent.

FREE TO HAVE YOUR SAY?

Journalists, bloggers, and Internet users have found that discussing certain topics can be dangerous. Sensitive subjects include ideas that conservatives might label "anti-Turkish." These include the legacy of Atatürk, the Kurdish question, religious issues, the role of the military, and radical activism. In 2013, the pianist and composer Fazıl Say, an outspoken critic of the Erdoğan government, was given a 10-month suspended jail term for having mocked certain religious practices on Twitter. In 2013, it was estimated that Turkey had more journalists in prison than any other country in the world.

Traditional housing mixes with new media. Satellite dishes are on many of the rooftops in Ankara.

Cellphone usage in Turkey is increasing— among old and young alike.

INTERNET ACCESS

The new communications media is overturning tradition, changing society, and raising all sorts of questions about rights and freedoms. Turkey has about 15.2 million landlines and 65 million mobile phones. As of 2012, there were 36 million Internet users. The main social media networks, such as Facebook, are popular. The government has censored the Internet for some years and blocked websites that it disapproves of, on political as well as moral grounds. That is a familiar story around the world, but new media is much harder to control than older forms.

ARTS, LEISURE, AND SPORTS

TURKISH ROOTS

Turkish music tradition is very different from that of Western Europe. Over the centuries it has interchanged with European and Middle Eastern cultures. With its origins in the Ottoman court, religious and military music is part of dancing and folk traditions. The literature, arts, and crafts of the Ottoman world are still celebrated. Examples include beautiful poetry, breathtaking architecture, art in miniature, elegant calligraphy (handwriting), precious inlaid woods, dazzling metalwork, embroidered textiles, patterned pottery, and tiles from the town of Iznik.

SOUND AND VISION

Many traditional influences and themes filter into contemporary music and arts. Mainstream pop in Turkey has had offshoots from rock to hip-hop and metal. In some cases, there is a fusion with folk roots. Turkey also has made its mark on the international art scene. Since the Istanbul Biennial show was set up in 1988, exciting new galleries have opened. All over the city, art is exhibited and is often striking, irreverent, and witty. Today's best known Turkish writers include Nobel Prize winner Orhan Pamuk (b.1952) and Elif Şafak (b.1971). Şafak is inspired not only by political change and the equality of women, but also by Turkey's long history of poetry and mysticism.

A rug is handwoven in the town of Göreme. Turkey has been known for its carpets and rugs for about 9,000 years.

NURi BiLGE CEYLAN'DAN

BiR ZAMANLAR ANADOLU'DA

MUHAMMET UZUNER   YILMAZ ERDOĞAN   TANER BiRSEL

Once Upon a Time in Anatolia is just one of the Turkish movies with recent success stories.

Galatasaray fans celebrate a goal during an away game in the Champions League competition.

MAKING MOVIES

Turkish movies date back to 1914 and were very popular from the 1950s to the 1970s. Today, there is a revival. Turkey produces more films than any European country other than France. Some Turkish filmmakers are highly respected. Director Semih Kaplanoglu's *Bal* picked up the Berlin Film Festival's Golden Bear in 2010. Nuri Bilge Ceylan's *Bir Zamaniar Anadolu'da* (*Once Upon a Time in Anatolia*) shared top prize at the Cannes Film Festival in 2011.

SPORTING ARENAS

Turkish weightlifters and wrestlers often perform impressively in international competitions. Wrestling by competitors smeared in olive oil is one of Turkey's traditional sports, and has its own rules and festivals. The big spectator sport in Turkey is soccer. Of five professional leagues, one is for women. Top teams, famous across Europe, include Fenerbahçe, Beşiktaş, and Galatasaray—who are said to have the loudest fans in the world!

FAITH AND FESTIVALS

A MUSLIM LAND

Islam is the prevailing religion in Turkey. The Islamic faith proclaims that there is one God (Allah) and that Muhammad is his prophet. Muslims must believe, pray five times daily, give charitably, fast during the month known in Turkish as Ramazan, and make a pilgrimage to Mecca (in Saudi Arabia). It has been claimed that 98 percent of all Turks are Muslim, but numbers and definitions are hard to pin down. Approximately 8 out of 10 Turkish Muslims follow the mainstream Sunni branch of the faith. Others are known as Alevi and follow an ancient Anatolian tradition. Alevism includes elements of the Shi'a branch of Islam, but it remains independent. Some declare that it is outside Islam altogether, as Alevi do not follow normal Muslim practices.

Friends in Istanbul gather before the start of the Islamic holy month of Ramazan. For the next month, they will not eat or drink during the hours of daylight.

The Christian church of the Holy Cross was built in 921 AD by the Armenian Apostolic Church. It is located on an island in Lake Van, in Eastern Turkey.

OTHER RELIGIONS

The very small religious minorities in Turkey, including Jews and Christians, belong to various eastern and western traditions. They have been tolerated for hundreds of years. Of these, only Jews, Armenians, and Greek Orthodox Christians have official recognition. The Turkish constitution remains secular.

WHIRLING MYSTICS

Alevi beliefs have elements of Sufism, a mystical practice in Islam. Mysticism in any religion is a way of approaching God through personal meditation or spiritual exercises. The Turkish Sufi order called the Mevlevi is based in the city of Konya. Members achieve a trance-like state by performing a dance to the chanting and music of drums and flute. Wearing white robes and tall hats that symbolize human mortality, they whirl around in ecstasy. This ritual was founded by Rumi, a great Persian poet of the 1200s, and may still be seen today.

IN CELEBRATION

Festivals mark the Turkish religious year. The end of the Islamic fasting period of Ramazan is called Şeker Bayramı (sugar feast). It is marked by three days of holiday, the giving of sweets, new clothes, shadow puppet shows, and visits to relatives. Secular holidays include New Year's Eve, which is celebrated with public fireworks displays, street performances, and parties. The founding of the Grand National Assembly is commemorated on April 23, which is a date that is also celebrated as International Children's Day with dancing, concerts, and sporting events. Republic Day (October 29) is the time for parades, flags, marching bands, and more fireworks.

The Sema, or ritual dance of the Mevlevi, is a remarkable form of religious experience.

One peaceful way to escape the hustle and bustle of Istanbul is to fish from the bridges or waterfront on a lazy sunny day. Old men can chat with their friends and bring home fresh mackerel.

FEASTING

Eating is a pleasure in this city, and meals are often served outdoors. Eggplant, peppers, olives, sheep's cheese, yogurt, mint, and rice are all common ingredients. Tasty snacks include vine leaves wrapped around rice, and *hummus*, a chickpea paste. Other favorites are soups; fresh seafood such as octopus or shrimps; and meatballs, lamb, or chicken kebabs. Sweets include *baklava* (pastries made with honey and pistachio), *halva* (crushed sesame seeds), *lokum* (jellies flavored with rosewater and nuts and known around the world as "Turkish delight"), and Istanbul's delicious milk and rice puddings.

CUP OF COFFEE?

The coffee shop was invented in Istanbul. The public sale of coffee was first recorded here as early as 1475. The Turkish version is brewed in a long-handled copper pot called an *ibrik*. It is served strong and thick. It is often drunk sweet and accompanied by a glass of cold water.

BATH TIME

Those in search of a healthier lifestyle visit a traditional *hamam* or Turkish bath. Public baths have been a part of city life for thousands of years. The baths offer combinations of hot and cold air with water and a vigorous massage with oil or soap.

SOCCER FANS

Sports fans cheered in the ancient city of Constantinople as teams battled in the chariot races at the Hippodrome. Today, soccer is the city's main sporting passion, with its local club, Fenerbahçe, as the stars. The city has four major stadiums and arenas.

ARTS AND CULTURE

Istanbul was declared Europe's "Capital of Culture" for 2010. At any time, it has rich cultural offerings, from the dazzling displays of Ottoman history in the Topkapi Palace to shows of cutting edge art at Istanbul Modern—the city's museum of modern art.

Spectacular fireworks light up the Bosphorus in celebration of Republic Day (October 29), which is a public holiday.

A fashionable dining spot in the Beyoğlu district offers fine views of the city and the Bosphorus.

The splendid Cağaloğlu Turkish baths were built in 1741 by Sultan Mahmud I. They are still open for use today.

As long as fish are swimming in the Golden Horn, Istanbul's anglers will be fishing on Galata Bridge.

TURKEY AND THE WORLD

AROUND THE WORLD

Turks do not just live in Turkey. Turkish communities are scattered around the globe, which creates useful connections with other nations, markets, and cultures. More than five million Turks live in Western Europe. Germany and the Netherlands recruited Turks as foreign workers from the 1960s onward. Many Turks also live in the Middle East and North America.

CYPRUS

The island of Cyprus has both Greek and Turkish populations which has led to 50 years of ethnic rivalry and division. In 1974, Northern Cyprus declared its independence as a separate Turkish state. Turkey invaded in support. This mini-state has never been recognized internationally.

ALLIANCES

Turkey has remained a member of NATO. Its geographical position between Europe, Russia, and the Middle East makes it a crucial ally of western governments. Turkey is in the Council of Europe and is an associate member of the EU. It applied for full membership in 2005. This is a slow process, but it has been delayed further by concerns within the EU about enlargement of the union. Turkey's European supporters say it would be a valuable addition as a bridge to the Middle East. Economic problems across Europe also have caused concern on all sides. However, the application has already had one result—encouraging democratic reform in Turkey.

Young Turks at this school in Duisburg, Germany, receive religious education in the Alevi tradition.

Israel has long been one of Turkey's regional allies. Relations were set back in 2010 by an Israeli attack on a ship carrying Turkish citizens protesting Israeli actions in Gaza.

FLASHPOINTS

The lands to the east and south of Turkey have been in a state of political turmoil for many decades. Iran has seen great political and religious upheavals, as has Iraq, and has been torn apart by years of war. Kurdish rebellions have crossed the borders. Turkey's relations with the former lands of the Ottoman empire, such as Egypt, are still very important. President Erdoğan and Prime Minister Davutoğlu may hope that a powerful and economically successful Turkey may regain a wider regional influence.

SYRIA

Since 2010, a wave of protests, uprisings, and civil wars have flared up across the Arab world. In 2011, Arab Spring reached Syria, Turkey's southern neighbor. Protests against the regime of Bashar al-Assad soon developed into a terrible conflict with many Syrian and international factions fighting the government. Clashes across the Turkish border include a Turkish jet being shot down and five Turks killed by Syrian army shellfire. Turkey has provided support to the rebels. More than 400,000 Syrians have fled into Turkey and are housed in 15 refugee camps.

Syrian refugees flee the fighting in Syria and camp at Reyhanlı on the Turkish side of the border.

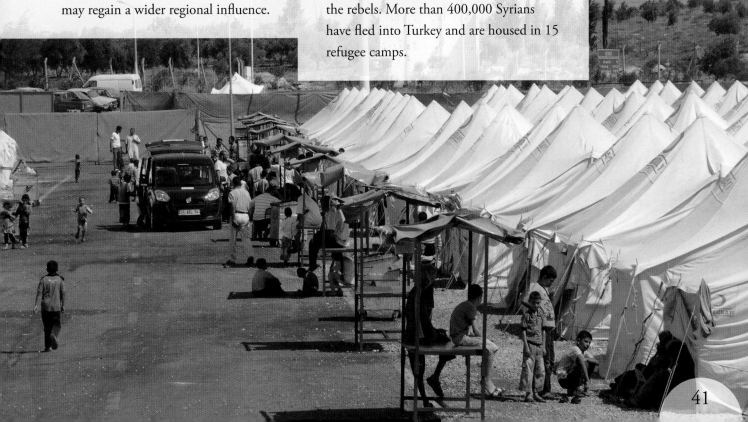

FACING THE FUTURE

SPECIAL CELEBRATION

In Turkey, weddings are important affairs and are preceded by meetings between the two families with the exchange of gifts. Many traditional customs may be honored, such as the decoration of the bride's hands with henna (temporary tattoos) and the wearing of a red ribbon, which is a symbol of virginity. The exchange of gifts, dancing, singing, and feasting can go on for days.

A PAUSE FOR THOUGHT

Whether the wedding is a traditional village gathering or a sophisticated city affair, it offers a chance for families to consider the past and look to the future. Most Turkish couples marry between the age of 17 and their early 20s. This generation will have been part of the great changes that their country has gone through in recent years. If they are fortunate, their family may have prospered from the economic upturn. If not, they may be struggling to pay their way.

IMPORTANT QUESTIONS

What kind of future can today's young Turkish people expect for their children? Can economic development be sustained? Will there be more or less equality between men and women, Turk and Kurd? Will human rights and democratic values be respected? Will society be secular or religious? Today's young people belong to the generation that will need to help decide these questions.

Just married! What does the future hold for these young Turkish people?

A TIME FOR HOPE

The view of Turkey as a bridge between western and eastern values is nothing new. This role has been a fact of life for thousands of years. For their own interests, modern Europeans and Asians need to respect this tradition and encourage it. But, of course, Turkey is more than just a bridge or a conduit. It is a remarkable nation in its own right. Turkey has a rich history and culture. Its people are known to be hardy and tough, talented and hospitable. These factors should give newlyweds hope for their children's future. An old Turkish proverb states, *"Çikmayan candan ümit kesilmez."* Its closest English equivalent? "As long as there is life, there is hope."

These refugees are Turkish Kurds who fled over the border to Iraq in the 1990s. The ongoing peace process gives them hope of returning home one day.

Sweeping plains and eroded rock formations are the backdrop of the new Turkey, a very ancient landscape.

GLOSSARY

Alevi a Turkish religious group that combines various Islamic traditions such as Sufism and some Shi'a beliefs

arable describing land that is suitable for growing crops

bazaar a market or shopping district, the Turkish word is *çarşı*

Byzantine Empire an empire that grew out of the Roman empire and lasted until 1453; largely Greek-speaking, its capital was Constantinople (today's Istanbul)

communist believing that the workers, or a party representing them, should be in charge of political and economic activity within a state

Constantinople a city founded by the Romans in 330 AD on the site of ancient Byzantium

constitution the laws, rules, and principles by which a country is governed

curriculum the program of learning within a school

deforestation the loss or destruction of forest and woodland

democratic a type of govrnment in which the people choose the leaders by voting

ecosystem an interactive community of living things within a particular environment

ethnic group people who share common descent, culture, customs, or language

ethnic Turk someone of the Turkish ethnic group

European Union (EU) an economic alliance of 28 nations

executive powers the authority to run the country

fossil fuel any carbon-based fuel such as coal, gas, or oil

free market an economic system based on supply and demand with little government control

gendarmerie a police force or militia

genocide the systematic extermination of a national or ethnic group

geothermal energy energy obtained from the inner heat of Earth

gross domestic product (GDP) a measure of wealth within a nation, region, or city often defined by the total amount spent on goods and services

honor killing the murder of a family member who is believed to have bought shame on the family

human rights a human's essential requirements for justice and equality

Kemalis a Turkish political movement based on the ideas of Mustafa Kemal Atatürk

manufacturing making raw materials into a finished product

minaret a tall, slender spire on a mosque that is used for calling Muslims to prayer

minority a smaller group within a larger one, such as a small ethnic group within a nation

mysticism seeking a direct consciousness of God, often through ritual or meditation

nationalist one who supports the creation of an independent or liberated nation, or believes in the superiority of one's own nation

NATO (North Atlantic Treaty Organization) a military alliance of 28 western nations

Ottoman (1) a branch of the Turkish people originally ruled by Osman I; (2) the name given to the Turks of Turkey and the empire they created

privatize handing over state-run enterprises to private companies

reprisal retaliation

republic a country with an elected head of state and government

rural in the countryside

secular non-religious

sedition stirring up opposition to a government

Seljuks a Turkish people who moved into the Middle East and conquered parts of the Byzantine empire in the Middle Ages

service industries industries that do not make things but provide services, such as banking, tourism, or catering

strait a narrow passage of water that connects two larger bodies of water

sultan a king or ruler of a Muslim state or country

sunken tunnel a tunnel that is not bored but is made from a series of tubes lowered from the surface

Turkic related to the wider groupings of Turks and their languages

urbanization the growth of towns and cities

FURTHER INFORMATION

BOOKS

Countries of the World: Turkey, Sarah Shields (National Geographic, 2009)

The Middle East, Philip Steele (Kingfisher Books, 2009)

WEBSITES

www.timemaps.com/history/turkey-1500bc
See the map of Turkey change through the ages from ancient times to the 21st century.

www.travel.nationalgeographic.com/travel/countries/turkey-facts/
A simple summary of facts about Turkey.

www.datesandevents.org/places-timelines/41-turkey-historical-timeline.htm
A timeline of Turkey's important people and events.

www.everyculture.com/To-Z/Turkey.html
Information on Turkey's history, economy, culture, clothing, customs, and more.

Every effort has been made by the publishers to ensure that the websites in this book are suitable for children, and that they contain no inappropriate or offensive material. However, because of the nature of the Internet, it is impossible to guarantee that the contents of these sites will not be altered. We strongly advise that Internet access is supervised by a responsible adult.

INDEX